This fun **Phonics** reader

belongs to

Ladybird Reading
Phonics
BOOK 11

Contents

A catalogue record for this book is available from the British Library

Published by Ladybird Books Ltd
80 Strand London WC2R 0RL
A Penguin Company

4 6 8 10 9 7 5 3
© LADYBIRD BOOKS LTD MMVI
LADYBIRD and the device of a Ladybird are trademarks of Ladybird Books Ltd

ISBN-13: 978-1-84646-316-7
ISBN-10: 1-84646-316-5

Printed in Italy

The Hairy Bear Scare

by Clive Gifford

illustrated by Stephen Holmes

introducing the **air** sound,
as in hair, bear, where and stare

When Clare came down
the stairs she had
a nasty scare.

For wherever she looked there were bears, bears, bears!

There were bears on the sofa
and bears on the chairs.

Would you care for a pear?

Hairy
Bear
Lair

There were bears
in the cupboard
underneath the stairs.

Clare stared at the bears.

The bears stared at Clare.

Clare's bear bared his teeth and glared.

"How dare you?" he growled. "This is MY lair!"

So off they ran those scared
hairy bears.

Dinosaur at the Door

by Naomi Adlington
illustrated by Karl Richardson

introducing the **or** sound, as in
morning, floor, before, claw, pause

One morning, George heard a knock at the door

and there on the doorstep he saw a huge dinosaur.

It held out its paw and said,
"Hi, my name is Jaws!

I'm awfully bored – will
you play with me outdoors?"

17

Poor George picked himself slowly off the floor.

He had only seen dinosaurs
in stories before.

George paused, then he looked at the dinosaur's claws.

"You can play on our lawn...

but *I'm* staying indoors!"

The Surfing Herd

by Clive Gifford
illustrated by Paula Knight

introducing the **er** sound,
as in surf, herd and swirl

What's that out there?
Oh, my word!

I can see a surfing herd!

They curve and swerve in the swirling surf.

They are so expert that they
never get hurt.

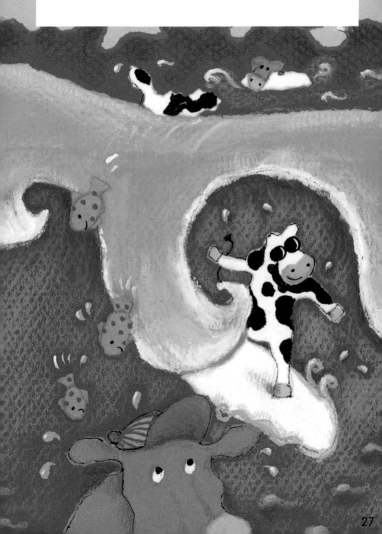

Watch how they turn with a
whoosh and a whirl,

riding the waves as they surge
through the swirl.

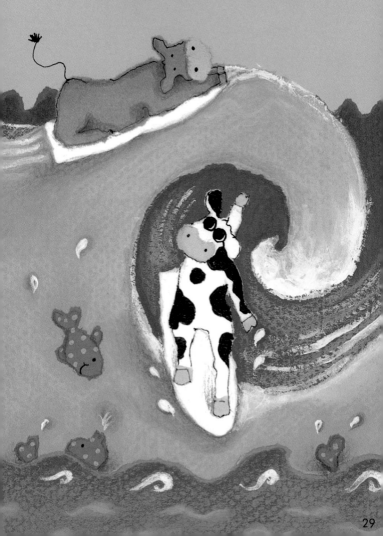

You won't find this herd grazing on turf.

These cool cows were born to surf.

HOW TO USE
Phonics
BOOK 11

This book introduces your child to the common spellings of the air, or and er sounds. The fun stories will help your child begin reading words including any of the common spelling patterns that represent these sounds.

- Read each story through to your child first. Familiarity helps children to identify some of the words and phrases.

- Have fun talking about the sounds and pictures together – what repeated sound can your child hear in each story?

- Help your child break new words into separate sounds (eg. l-aw-n) and blend their sounds together to say the word.

- Point out how words with the same written ending sound the same. If s-urf says 'surf', what does t-urf say?

- Some common words, such as 'what', 'said' and even 'the', can't be read by sounding out. Help your child practise recognising words like these.

Phonic fun

Playing word games with your child is a fun way to build her phonic skills. Try playing rhyming I-Spy, using words with the air, er, or er sound in. Or challenge your child to think of as many words with a particular sound in them as they can in a minute.

Ladybird Reading
Phonics

Phonics is part of the Ladybird Reading range. It can be used alongside any other reading programme, and is an ideal way to practise the reading work that your child is doing, or about to do in school.

Ladybird has been a leading publisher of reading programmes for the last fifty years. **Phonics** combines this experience with the latest research to provide a rapid route to reading success.

The fresh quirky stories in Ladybird's twelve **Phonics** storybooks are designed to help your child have fun learning the relationship between letters, or groups of letters, and the sounds they represent.

This is an important step towards independent reading – it will enable your child to tackle new words by sounding out and blending their separate parts.

How Phonics works

- The stories and rhymes introduce the most common spellings of over 40 key sounds, known as phonemes, in a step-by-step way.

- Rhyme and alliteration (the repetition of an initial sound) help to emphasise new sounds.

- Bright amusing illustrations provide helpful picture clues and extra appeal.